The Hollywell Family

MARGARET KORNITZER

Illustrated by Shirley Hughes

The Bodley Head

LONDON   SYDNEY

TORONTO

2

Robert and Freda Hollywell were husband and wife and they lived in a little house with a big garden all round it. Downstairs there was a bright kitchen with red tiles on the floor, and upstairs there were three bedrooms and a bathroom with fishes painted round the walls.

Not many months after Robert and Freda had moved into their new house they knew that Freda was going to have a baby and they were very pleased. They wanted a family of two, a girl and a boy. They didn't mind which came first.

Freda said, "I'm sure it will be a boy."

Robert said, "I am sure it will be a girl."

"It doesn't matter a bit," they both said at once.

"Which of the two spare bedrooms shall we get ready for the new baby?" said Freda.

"The one with the apple tree outside," said Robert. "I'll paint the walls yellow and the door and window-frames white."

"And I'll make white curtains with yellow ducks printed on them," said Freda.

Soon everything was ready and the baby was born. It was a girl. She was just what Robert and Freda wanted and they were delighted with her. At first the baby had no hair at all but soon it started to grow. Robert and Freda called the baby Mary.

Mary kicked a lot and made gurgling noises, but she couldn't talk and she didn't have any teeth to bite with, so she was only given milk at first.

Robert was Mary's Daddy, and Freda was Mary's Mummy. There were now three people in the Hollywell Family—Daddy, Mummy and Mary.

When Mary was nearly a year old she began to walk, then to talk. She said, "Dad, Dad", and then she said, "Mum, Mum." She had some nice white teeth and could eat all sorts of things.

She grew tall and strong and soon she was
two years old—and then she was three.

Daddy and Mummy thought
she was wonderful. They loved
her more and more.

One day Daddy said, "Wouldn't it be lovely if Mary had a little brother or sister?"

Mummy thought so too. "It would be lovely," she said.

So they hoped and waited. They waited a long time. But no baby was born. The doctor told them they would not be able to have another baby.

"Oh dear," said Daddy and Mummy, "what shall we do?"

"Yes, what *shall* we do?" said Mary, who was now getting to be a big girl. "I would like to have a baby brother to play with."

"Perhaps there's a baby somewhere who needs us?" said Mummy. "If we found the right baby we could adopt him."

"What does that mean?" asked Mary.

Daddy explained. "Some babies are born to people who can't take care of them, and then somebody has to find them new mummies and daddies who can look after them. That's called adoption. Perhaps *we* shall be given a baby to love as our own? Then you will have your baby brother, Mary."

"Denis Smith was adopted by his Mummy and Daddy. He told me so," said Mary. Denis was a boy who lived two houses up the road.

"Yes, that's right," said Daddy. "Well—now we know that we all want a baby we had better start looking for one."

"Where shall we start?" said Mary, standing on her tiptoes with excitement.

"I think Daddy and I will go and ask the doctor first," said Mummy.

Next morning when Mary was at school Daddy and Mummy went to ask Doctor Brown about adopting a baby. The doctor thought it was a very good idea.

"What does Mary think about it?" he asked.

"Mary can't wait to have a baby brother," said Mummy.

"The question is," said Daddy, "where do we look for a baby?"

"It's a good question," said Doctor Brown. "Babies are very precious and there aren't many wanting a home and new parents. If I were you I would go and ask Mrs Poppett what *she* thinks. Mrs Poppett is the lady who knows all about adopting babies."

Daddy and Mummy went home and told Mary what the doctor had said.

"Let's go and see Mrs Poppett *now*," said Mary.

"I think we'll wait until tomorrow," said Mummy. "Why don't you paint a picture of a baby for me?"

So Mary painted a picture of a baby. Then she drew a cot, and after that she drew a pram. "I'll keep the pictures to show the baby when he comes," she said.

The next day they all piled into the car and off they went to
see Mrs Poppett. She had an office in the Town Hall.

"We have come to see Mrs Poppett about adopting a baby,"
Daddy said to the man at the desk by the door.

"Just wait a minute, please." The man spoke into a telephone.
"Mr and Mrs Hollywell to see you about adoption, Mrs
Poppett."

The man turned to the Hollywell family. "You are to go
straight up. Follow those stairs, turn to the right and then to
the left and Mrs Poppett's name is on the door."

"I am going to have a baby brother," said Mary to the man
as they left.

"Just fancy," said the man. "Good for you!"

Mrs Poppett was sitting at a big table. The wall behind her was covered with pictures of babies. She smiled at Mary and turned to Mr Hollywell. "What can I do for you?"

"We want to adopt a little brother for Mary," said Daddy.

"And do *you* want a baby brother?" said Mrs Poppett to Mary.

"Oh, yes, yes, I do," said Mary. "Is he here?"

"No," said Mrs Poppett and smiled. "You know there are not many babies who want to be adopted just now but we'll have to see what we can do."

"I'd like that one," said Mary, pointing to one of the photographs.

Mrs Poppett laughed. "Oh, he's been adopted long ago. Now he's as big as you are. First of all, I would like to ask you some questions, Mr and Mrs Hollywell, so that I can start looking."

Mrs Poppett took out a long piece of paper and wrote down what Daddy and Mummy told her. They told her all about their house and about the empty room that was just waiting for a baby.

After she had finished asking questions Mrs Poppett said, "Well, I'll have to let you know. Just as soon as I hear of the right baby for you I'll tell you, I promise. Then Mary will have a brother. But I'm afraid you may have to wait quite a long time."

Mary was very disappointed and just stared out of the car window all the way home.

"I don't expect it will be very long, Mary," said Mummy comfortingly when they got back. "The time will soon go and I'm counting on you to help me get everything ready for the new baby."

"There's a lot to do," said Daddy. "I have to paint the spare room. What colours shall we have?"

"Green!" said Mary, skipping up and down in her excitement.

"And I'll make some pink curtains with white chickens all
over them," said Mummy.

"I'll paint a picture for the baby," said Mary. So she did. It
was a picture of a daddy elephant and a mummy elephant with
two baby elephants.

"The baby will be pleased with that," said Mummy.

"We'll have to buy a new pram and a new bath," said Daddy.

"And a special soft hairbrush, and vests and baby lotion, and all sorts of other things," said Mummy.

They made a long list of all the things the baby would need.

"You can pay for them with some of the money in my piggy bank," said Mary.

"That will be very useful," said Daddy. "Thank you."

The time seemed to Mary to pass very slowly but one day Daddy and Mummy had a letter from Mrs Poppett. She wrote, "There is a lovely baby waiting for you in the baby nursery at Newtown, just a few miles from you. Please go and see him quickly. Matron will be waiting for you."

"We'll go straight away," said Daddy. "How lucky it's Saturday and I don't have to go to work!" He went to get the car ready, and Mummy took out of a drawer a set of baby clothes and a beautiful big white shawl that she had knitted for the baby. Mary took her favourite one-eyed Teddy Bear with her, for company.

22

After a short drive they came to a tall house with a fine cherry tree in full flower in the front garden. They all went inside, Daddy, Mummy, Mary and Teddy. There was a lot of noise of babies.

"Do you suppose one of those babies is our baby?" said Mary.

"Perhaps!" said Mummy.

They were shown into a room and asked to wait. Mary couldn't sit still. She hugged Teddy and whispered in his ear, "Our baby is coming! Do be quiet and wait!"

Just at that moment the door opened and in came Matron carrying a baby.

"Come and look!" said Matron. She sat down in an easy chair
with the baby in her lap.

They crowded round her. Mummy knelt down and Matron
turned the shawl back and showed them the baby's face. He was
fast asleep.

"His name is George," said Matron.

"What a nice name," said Mummy.

"He looks like a George," said Daddy. "He's splendid, isn't he!"

"I think he's lovely," said Mary, standing on tiptoe to see better.

They all thought he was a most beautiful baby.

"Can we take him home with us *now*?" asked Mummy.

"Of course," said Matron. "I hoped you would love him straight away."

"George can have my Teddy when he wakes up," said Mary. "Can he play with me then?"

"Not yet," said Mummy. "He's much too small. He's got to grow. Will you help me to look after him?"

"Oh, yes," said Mary. "I know just how."

So all four of them went home in the car.

When they put George into his new cot he woke up. He had large dark brown eyes, and he gave Mary a big smile.

"Do you suppose he knows he is my brother?" asked Mary.

"It looks like it," said Daddy.

Daddy and Mummy and Mary were delighted with George. He was exactly the little boy they all wanted.

"Where did George come from?" Mary asked.

"Don't you remember what Daddy told you about adopting a baby?" said Mummy. "George had another Mummy and Daddy to begin with, but they couldn't look after him, so they asked Mrs Poppett to find some people like us who would adopt him."

"Aren't we lucky!" said Mary.

"Yes," said Mummy. "George is very precious. Somebody will come soon to make sure we are looking after him properly."

Sure enough, one day a lady came to visit them. "I've been sent to see if George is happy and if everything is all right," she said to Mary.

"Of course it is!" said Mary. "He's my brother!"

"I can see how you love him," the lady said. "Won't it be wonderful when he is old enough to play with you!"

The lady had been sent by the court. After a few more visits she said, "Now it is time for you to go and see the Judge so that George can be made truly yours."

In a few days they all went to court to adopt George before the Judge. Daddy and Mummy and Mary and George sat in front of the Judge's big desk. The Judge handed Daddy an important-looking piece of paper. "This is the adoption order," he said. "It confirms that the baby is properly adopted. Nobody can take George away from you now."

The Judge shook hands with them all. Mary felt very grown up.

Now there were four people in the Hollywell Family—
Daddy and Mummy and Mary and George. They all
lived happily together in the little house with the big
garden all round it.

Text © Margaret Kornitzer 1973 Illustrations © The Bodley Head 1973 ISBN 0 370 01147 3
Printed in Great Britain for The Bodley Head Ltd, 9 Bow Street, London WC2E 7AL
by William Clowes & Sons Ltd, Beccles
Colour separations by Colourcraftsmen Ltd, Chelmsford
First published 1973